Edo Manga Double Issue!

仙傳延壽反魂談

Help! A Ninja Stole My Soul!

三千歳成云蚺蛇

The Great Serpent Turns 3,000 Years Old

山東京伝著
Story & Art: SANTO KYODEN
細田栄之絵
Art: HOSODA EISHI
シャハン・エリック訳
Translation: ERIC SHAHAN

Portrait of Kyoden when he was around 30
by Hosoda Eri
細田栄里

Origins of Edo Manga

In the early 1600s the tumultuous Warring States Period ended. These near endless wars had raged since 1467 were finally resolved to establish the beginnings of the peaceful Edo Era. Freed from constant war, average citizens became able to work and trade freely within the bounds of the feudal system. Literacy rates began to rise as the emerging merchant class sent their children to temple schools and private tutors. With a higher rate of literacy a market in mass produced books and pamphlets emerged, and in the 1660s a new kind of book emerged called *Kusazōshi* 草双紙 "grass leaves books" or Edo Manga. The early Edo Manga were adventure tales geared towards women and children, who had become literate due to attending Terakoya (temple schools), however they soon became popular with a wider range of people. This resulted in more sophisticated stories with elaborate art and layouts, eventually becoming sarcastic critiques of modern society. The audience switched from women and children to Samurai households and literary people. Eventually the popularity of the Edo Manga reached the Edo-ko, a name referring to Edo city dwellers, and the books became a standard type of pulp-fiction. The genre survived until the beginning of the Meiji Era in 1868 and the advent of modern printing presses to Japan.

Evolution

Both the style and content of Edo Mana changed over time and researchers have categorized them by the color of the outer cover which changed as the style evolved. The covers of the books went from red, black, blue and finally yellow. At each stage the stories became more complex and expanded in length as the art became more sophisticated and the stories more complex. The earliest *Kusazōshi,* red covered books, were single stories while later yellow-cover books could be up to ten parts, split into 20 books. Each part of the story would be sold separately. Later, the multiple parts of the book would be bound into single volume. This is similar to how modern Japanese manga are sold first a chapter at a time in weekly magazines and then later compiled into a book.

The illustration above by Settan Hasegawa (1778–1843)長谷川雪旦 shows the *Lucky Crane House Uemon* 鶴屋喜右衛門 bookshop in Edo. This is a Local Book Shop 地本問屋 that sold illustrated Edo Manga as well as Ukiyo-e Floating World prints of heroes, actors and landscapes.

Earlier books were unattributed while later books attributed both the names of the writer and artist. Also the original adventure stories and simple fairy tales gave way to abbreviated versions of Kabuki plays and classic stories. Eventually the Kibyōshi 黄表紙 (yellow cover) style Edo Manga began satirically to reference contemporary figures and contemporary Japanese society. However, a series of strict censorship laws beginning in 1791 ended political satire and publications were prohibited from discussing current events and politics. Government censors decreed all printed matter had to be reviewed and approved before publication; approved publications carried a detailed notice of the censors' approval. Sanctions against publishing unapproved material were draconian, which caused the writers and artists to switch to tales of morality or stories of revenge.

How were they made?

Each book is usually five woodblock prints sewn together. One story typically consists of three books for a total of 15 pages, though some are longer or shorter. The Hiragana Japanese phonetic syllabary was used with few Kanji, making them very readable.

Who read them?

The Samurai class, about 7% of the population, was literate; however, starting in the 17th century the expanding merchant class also began to educate their children. In Edo, today's Tokyo and the home base of the ruling Tokugawa *Bakufu* military government, the literacy rate was estimated to have been around 80% for males and 25 % for females, compared with the national average of 40-50% overall. Edo Manga as a form of popular literature, were targeted mainly to women and children; however, they were undoubtedly read by Samurai (albeit perhaps covertly.)

Are they hard to translate?

Japanese is already one of the more difficult languages to learn, in fact, according to the US State Department's Foreign Service Institute, modern Japanese is the most difficult language for a native English speaker to acquire basic fluency. Edo Era (1603-1868) Japanese is even more difficult, written in archaic style heavily influenced by ancient written Chinese and these books include witty and ironic commentary on contemporary society. The original script is a special type of handwritten, cursive Japanese that is illegible even to most educated Japanese today. Despite years of practice I often cannot fully read the original text in most Edo Manga; however, transcriptions of the text into standard Japanese letters are available. Though these books help in reading the text, the language and humor is still very much from the 17th~19th century Japan.

Even the arrangement of text and illustrations on one page is a bit of an adventure in itself, as it is not always clear who is saying what, when and in what order. In a sense it doesn't matter and I suspect that contemporary readers likely enjoyed piecing the story of each scene together.

An example of one of the five, two-page spreads that make up an Edo Manga. The text starts on the right and flows to the left. It can be difficult to determine which part to read first.

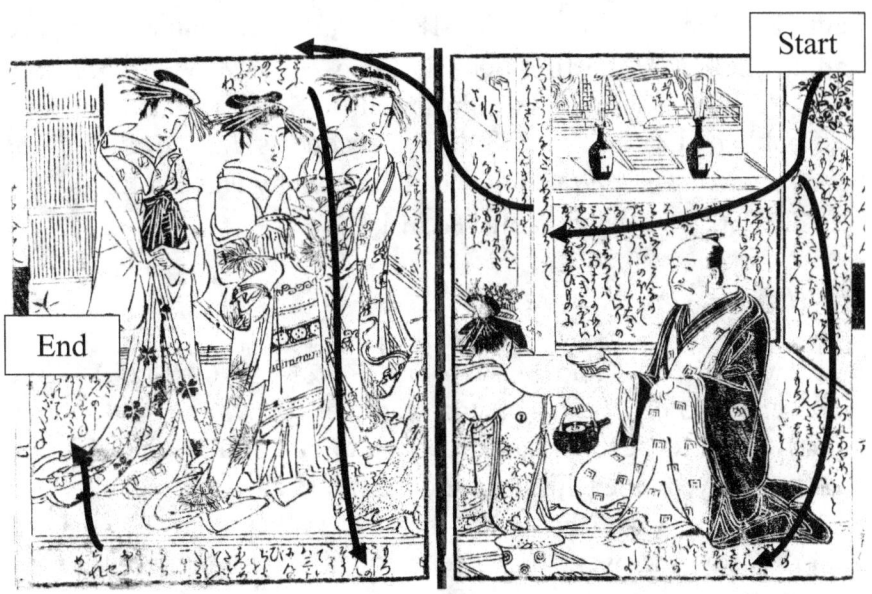

In order to keep the two page spreads together it was sometimes necessary to add an extra page in the middle of the story. I used this as an opportunity to use these extra pages to add more background information regarding concepts, characters, and unfamiliar items used in the stories.

About this Edo Manga Double Issue:

This Edo Manga Double issue contains two works written by Santo Kyoden 山東京伝 (1761-1816) whose real name was Iwase Samuru 岩瀬醒. The first book is titled *Help! A Ninja Stole My Soul!* It is both written and illustrated by Santo Kyoden and was first published in Edo in 1789. The second is *The Great Serpent Turns 3,000 Years Old* which was illustrated by Hosoda Eishi 細田栄之, (1756~1829) and published in 1787.

- *Help! A Ninja Stole My Soul!*

The art is by Kitao Masayoshi 北尾政美 (1764-1824.) While relatively unknown today, Kitao was well known in at the time. Iwase (Santo Kyoden) was apprenticed to him at the age of 13, and took the Ukiyo name Kitao Masanobu 北尾政演. He used this when he illustrated works (the second book is an example.) His master, Kitao Masayoshi, went on to reinvent his style and changed his name to Kuwada Keisai 鍬形蕙斎. There was even a popular phrase that went *I hate Hokkusai but love Keisai* 北斎嫌いの蕙斎好き.

Help! A Ninja Stole My Soul! was published in three volumes of five pages, with two illustrations on each page, for a total of 30 pages.

The story is a critique of the idle rich who Santo may have interacted with. Through his story of everyday life he shows the kinds of things that went on in everyday society in Edo during the 18th century. During this period Japan was closed to foreigners for the most part with only select ports open for international trade.

- *The Great Serpent Turns 3,000 Years Old*

This book was illustrated by Hosoda Eishi 細田栄之, (1756~1829) and published in 1787. It places supernatural creatures in everyday settings similar to *The Diary of Lord Fudo of Three River Island* (which I translated in Edo Manga #2 but was published later in 1789.) It consists of two volumes of five double-panels, for a total of 20 pages, so it is shorter than other works.

Note on the contemporary cost:

In Edo a single issue would sell for about 6-8 Mon (pennies.) Converting this to modern prices is a bit tricky, but scholars have used the price of food at a lunch stall as a marker. At the time the cheapest meal you could buy was Kake- Soba (soba noodles with seaweed or other toppings) that cost about 16 Mon. Based on that it seems one issue would cost between 100-200¥, which is about 1-2$.

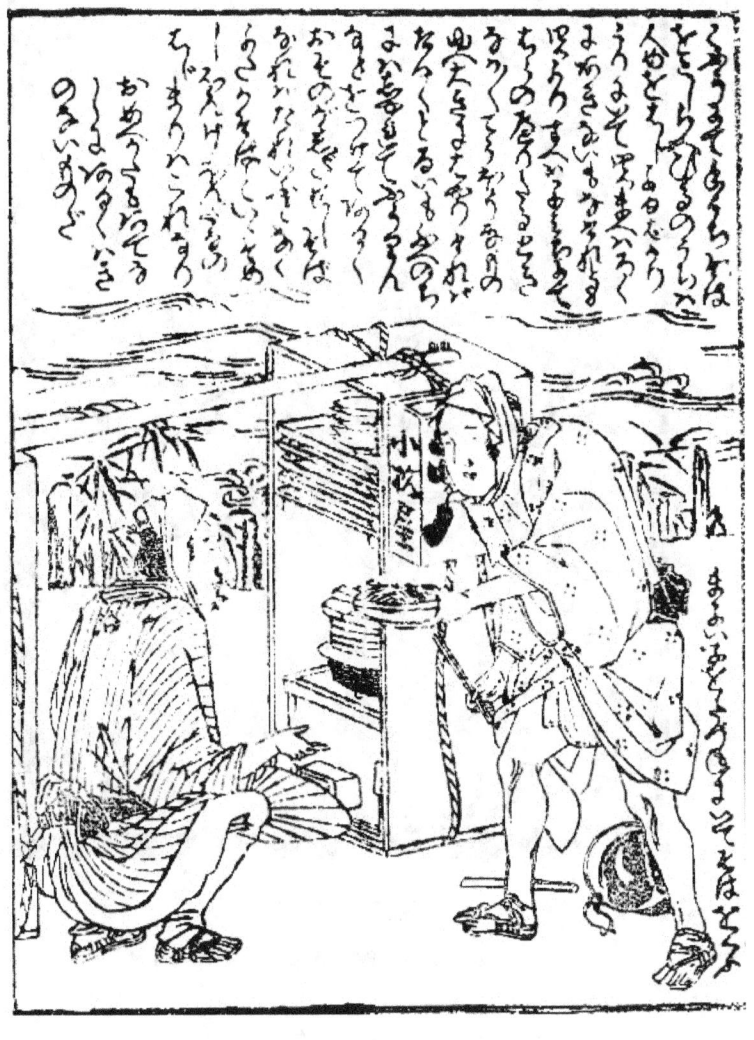

A patron purchasing Soba noodles from a portable stall.

Help! A Ninja Stole My Soul!
The story of a man with just a month left to live.

Cover of Volume 1 of 3

仙傳延壽反魂談

Help! A Ninja Stole My Soul!
The story of a man with just a month left to live.

Note: A more direct translation of this title is:

As Prescribed by Taoist Immortals,
A Medicine for Eternal Live and Reanimating the Dead

Story by: Santo Kyoten 山東京伝
Illustrated by: Kitao Masanobu 北尾政演
(The Ukiyo artist name of Santo Kyoten. In other words, he is the writer and artist.)

Help! A Ninja Stole My Soul!
Book 1

Chapter 12 of *The Analects of Confucius*（論語）is titled *The Master's Answers Philanthropy Friendships*（顔淵.）　We find the line, *Life and death are at the discretion of the heavens, humans do not have the power to control them.*

This tells us humans can build wealth for themselves and improve their status, however this is solely due to the grace of heaven. Without the blessing of the God Tentei 天帝 (Considered to be the "Primordial Deity" or "First Deity" in Classical Chinese) no matter how much you hope it will not happen.

However, the God Tentei is not just involved in granting wealth and status but also the administration of the lifespan of humans. Every man, woman and child has their name recoded in great book. For those whose allotted lifespan has ended Tentei adds a mark to their name with his brush. He keeps his ledger book much like the owner of a pawnshop does.

One evening as the sun was going down Tentei was very busy and he accidentally erased part of his ledger. When he was rewriting it he inadvertently added a mark above the name of a certain Ichikawa Shosuke. While this may have been bad for him it resulted in a mountain of good material which I, the author, plan to make good use of.

Note:

The full quote from *The Analects* is:

The same disciple, being in trouble, remarked, "I am alone in having no brother, while all else have theirs younger or elder."

Tsz-hi said to him, "I have heard this: 'Death and life have destined times; wealth and honors rest with Heaven. Let the superior man keep watch over himself without ceasing, showing deference to others, with propriety of manners and all within the four seas will be his brethren. How should he be distressed for lack of brothers!"

From *The Analects* published 1900. Translated by William Jennings (1847 – 1927.)

It was early spring in Edo and the man known as Ichikawa Shosuke felt the days in this time of year were too long. Being somewhat bored he lunged and took a nap. While he was doing that his soul took the opportunity to float about and play

Just then Iwato Kagura music began to emanate from somewhere and suddenly a black clad Ninja leapt onto the scene.

The Ninja snatched Shosuke's soul and fled.

Just by chance Ichikawa's friend Kaneko was stopping by to offer a seasonal greeting. He arrived just as the Ninja was turning to leave. For a moment their eyes met by the light of Ichikawa's stolen soul. It lasted no longer than a heartbeat, then the Ninja was gone.

In his sleep Ichikawa Shosuke shouted:

Stop you bastard cheat!
Its Kozo (Nezumi Kozo) someone call the police! Call them!

Ninja:

My mission was completely successful I am grateful indeed!

Notes:

Kagura 神楽 means entertaining the gods. In this case, Shinto gods. Iwami Kagura is the type of dance done in western Shimane Prefecture. The origin of Kagura is not known but it is described in the Kojiki written in the 8th century. This ceremony is done to pray for a bountiful harvest and to ward off natural (earthquakes) and supernatural (giant snakes) disasters. In the story, Amaterasu Okami (God of the Sun) hides behind a rock. Many gods dance and play music hoping to coax her out to shine light on the world again. Some notable features of Iwami Kagura are fast-paced music and dance, gorgeous costumes and simple stories. The music is played with small drums and flutes.

http://www.all-iwami.com/en/kagura/wk/

Nezumi Kozō "Rat Boy" (鼠小僧) is the nickname of Nakamura Jirokichi (仲村次郎吉, 1797 - 1831),a Japanese thief who later became a folk hero. He is said to have stolen 30,000 gold coins over a 15 year period, all from guarded Samurai estates. In 1822, he was caught and tattooed, and banished from Edo. He went on to burgle Samurai households in Edo for another decade before being captured. He was paraded around town on a horse before being beheaded. His severed head was displayed for 3 days. He was buried at Eko-in Temple near the Ryogoku neighborhood of Tokyo.
The Ninjutsu researcher Soryu Ken 双竜軒 wrote about Nezumi Kozo in The Secret Magic of Ninjutsu 忍術魔法秘伝：神秘開放 変化自由, published in 1917.

Anytime you visit the grave of Nezumi-kozo you will find incense burning. There is never a time when this is not so. (His grave is in the Ryogoku section of Tokyo.) Such devotion to a figure is typically only seen around the graves of the virtuous 47 Ronin. The reason behind this is the fact that Nezumi-Kozo had received enlightenment in the arts known as Ninjutsu.

When Shosuke finally woke up he only stared listlessly in one direction. This is because his soul had been taken from his body. He was as bland as a soup made with old trimmings of dried bonito and boiling water. Shosuke was like a carp streamer hanging limply on a windless day. It was like he was a man without a heartbeat.

Secretary:
I can't imagine what the master has been dwelling on all afternoon. His whole manner is quite strange, I don't recall him being bitten by a fox.

Note: Foxes were considered magical creatures that played tricks on humans and could shapeshift. This is the first time I have read of foxes biting people.

Shosuke's condition did not improve and he had less and less interest in the world around him. To remedy this he called the famous physiognomist Kantsuken for an evaluation.

Note: A Physiognomist is a person that practices the art of physiognomy, or assessing a person's character or personality from their outer appearance—especially the face.

Kantsuken observed Shosuke carefully and what he saw crushed his liver (astonished him.)
You, my young friend, have had your soul stolen from you! On the 3rd of next month you will most certainly die. He followed up this disheartening news with, *If you have anything you want to say you had better say it quickly.*
A physiognomist is just like any other person, and they judge people based on the 32 Characteristics of a Great Man.

When people borrow money they are pleasant as Jizo roadside shrines, when it comes time to collect debts people become the devil. When their eyes droop at the corners they are giving a good reading, if their nose is up in the air they are heaping praise on their client. Those with frizzy hair give good readings, those with red cheeks give smelly readings, and of course there are many variations of this.

You know what your problem is? You are rich but you handle yourself badly and that is why this happened. You made it easy for that Ninja to steal your soul. You need to be more aware. Kansuken advised him.

Note:
The 32 Characteristics of a Great Man are how the Buddha is supposed to be depicted. Prior to the 2nd century CE there weren't any statues of the Buddha.

1. He has feet with a level sole.
2. He has the mark of a thousand-spoked wheel on the soles of his feet
3. He has projecting heels
4. He has long fingers and toes.
5. His hands and feet are soft-skinned
6. He has netlike lines on palms and soles
7. He has high raised ankles
8. He has taut calf muscles like an antelope
9. He can touch his knees with the palms of his hands without bending.
10. His sexual organs are concealed in a sheath
11. His skin is the color of gold
12. His skin is so fine that no dust can attach to it
13. His body hair are separate with one hair per pore
14. His body hair are blue-black, the color of collyrium, and curls clockwise in rings.
15. He has an upright stance like that of a Brahma
16. He has the seven convexities of the flesh
17. He has an immense torso, like that of a lion
18. The furrow between his shoulders is filled in
19. The distance from hand-to-hand and head-to-toe is equal
20. He has a round and smooth neck
21. He has sensitive taste-buds
22. His jaw is like that of lion.
23. He has a nice smile
24. His teeth are evenly spaced
25. His teeth are without gaps in-between
26. His teeth are quite white
27. He has a large, long tongue
28. He has a voice like that of a Brahma
29. He has very blue eyes
30. He has eyelashes like an ox
31. He has a white soft wisp of hair in the center of the brow
32. His head is like a royal turban

Shosuke thought deeply about his situation and he finally grasped that his time on Earth was limited and he would die next month.

Startled by this realization he thought, *Soon the floating world will be more than just a dream.* And, becoming flustered he continued, *All this time I have been very frugal but it turns out to have served me badly! I don't have any children to turn my wealth over to...*

Shosuke decided that it would not be wise to leave any money behind. He decided to liquidate his assets and spend every last penny. He proceeded to sell his house, property and all his furniture without exception. In addition, he summoned his secretary, butler, maid and even the cook. After handing each an appropriate number of gold coins he released them from his service.

Butler:

Though we were not born in Edo, leaving such a great master is truly a tragedy.

His now former secretary said,

May no shadow of misfortune ever befall you!

Then burst into hysterical crying.

Shosuke: *You all may take your leave as soon as you have packed your things.*

Maid:
With all these men with Chonmage Samurai hairstyles lined up it looks like we are going to start a million prayer chant to the Buddha.

Note: 百万遍念仏
Chanting one million prayers to the Buddha is done for your own salvation, for a person that has already passed away or other reasons. If done by one person it can take 7-10 days, however groups 10 people, with each person doing 10,000 prayers is another way to achieve one million prayers in one day.

All the retainers of the Ichikawa household returned to their lodging house.

The butler sat down on a rock and sighed,
There is no road ahead for us…We are being changed out, like the set pieces in the 4th act of the 47 Ronin Puppet play. Or maybe we are like a slip of paper forgotten in the drawer of the company's ledger box.

Cover of Volume 2 of 3

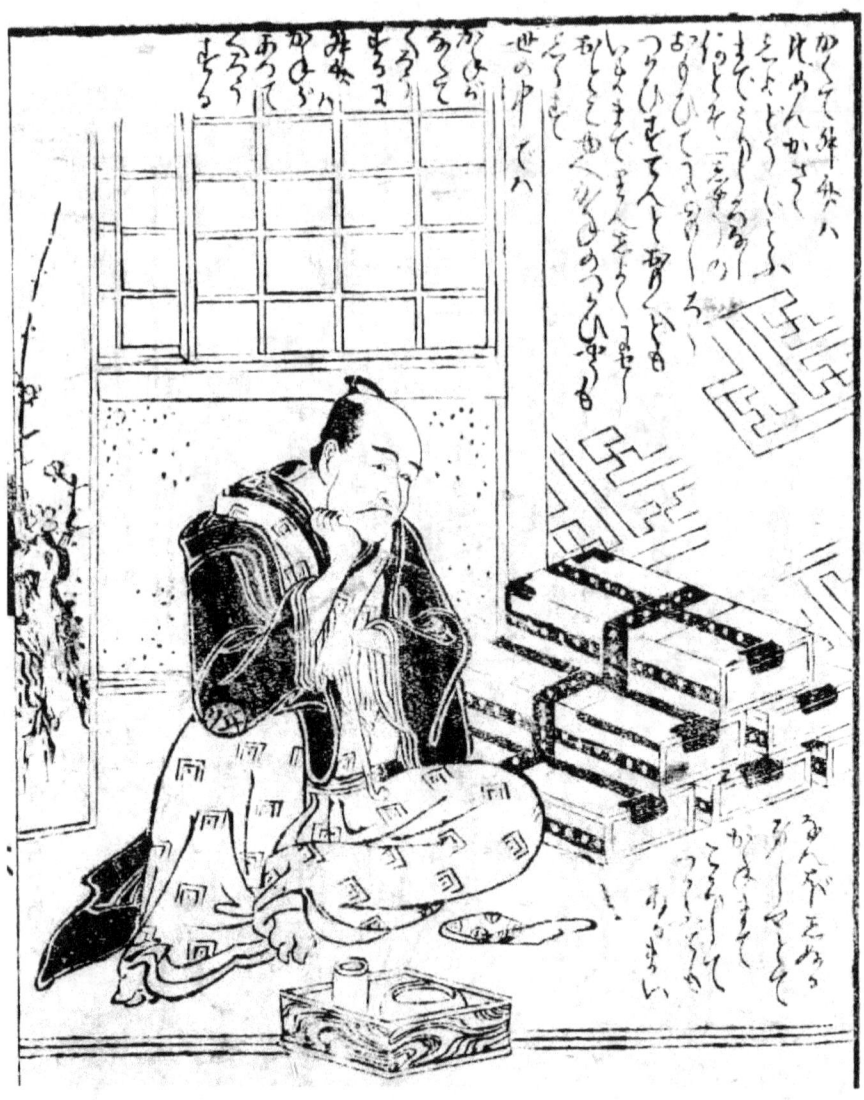

Shosuke, having sold his home, property, all his furniture and even his staff and servants, realized that everything he had accumulated in his life was now gone.

"I have lived rather a dull life..." he thought. Since Shosuke spent his days being frugal, even miserly he had no idea how to spend money. While there are many people in the world suffering from a lack of money, Shosuke was suffering despite having money. *Even though I have a death sentence hanging over my head I have to kill off my money somehow.*

Shosuke's first notion was to spend a thousand gold coins on a grand night in the Yoshiwara pleasure district. He used the money to rent out an entire house in the district. Inside a fur rug was spread out and the entire rom filled with courtesans. Taiko drum players and local Geisha provided entertainment and it soon became a loud, wild affair.

Though Shosuke could see the decadence around him he was unable to muster any enthusiasm for the excitement going on around him. So the host of the party seemed to be playing a minor role in the soiree. The sound of all the boisterous music, laughter and talking started to give Shosuke a headache.

Then came the hardest task of the evening…going to bed. With 3,000 courtesans in tow he made his way to the bed house. The procession looked the same as one of those wealthy women going Kimono shopping go by buying everything in sight. As he looked all the courtesans over he found he was unable to make a decision.

Well it looks like renting out a whole place in the pleasure district was a bust…rather boring in the end.

Courtesan 1:
I feel like an iris flower, suffering after it has been plucked. I don't understand…This guy should have gone to Kichijoji temple instead.

Note: The first Kanji of Kichijoji temple 吉祥寺 is the same as the first Kanji of Yoshiwara 吉原, though the pronunciation is different.)

Courtesan 2:
Who should I offer this cup of Sake to? If I invite him to have a drink he won't invite me to make love…

Courtesan 3 to another Courtesan:
Would you trade places with me? I think he doesn't like me.

Courtesan 2:
I'm not sure what I should say.

Courtesan 4:
What is with this old geezer? He doesn't act at all like a lord.
They say the Chinese Emperor Genso Kotei gathered 3,000 beautiful women, but then again it probably took his whole life to see each of them.

Note:
Emperor Xuanzong of Tang 685-762 CE 武隆基 had 50 children by concubines. It seems the number 3000 is low as Wikipedia and other sources say he kept 40,000 concubines.

Shosuke's next idea was to spend 1000 gold coins renting out a theater for a day. Since he was the only audience member there was no one to shout out,

Attention Please! Ichikawa is here, Attention, a young master is lavishing us with his presence. And other such praise.

There were no people shouting out *Manju!* (a steamed bun with a sweet filling) *Okoshi!* (A rice cake mixed with peanuts, covered with sugar and roasted.) *Knitted goods! Naga Uta* (epic songs!) *Programs! Get your programs!*

No one was attaching orange peel to strips of paper and throwing them.

No one shouted out *The Kojo* 口上 *is beginning!* (Prologue at the start of a kabuki performance)*!*

At the moment the curtain rises, no one shouted with feverish anticipation,

He hasn't taken the stage yet!

The whole day, just before the Kyogen performance no one shouted,

We've been waiting!

This is what we came for!

And afterwards shouting,

That was fantastic! Just the right amount!

You resemble your father! (Actors have hereditary roles)

However, Shosuke found himself happy seeing the Kyogen and let out a breath having been entertained. He was then invited to the tea house to meet the actors. He sat with all the actors right in front of him.

When one actor dressed as a woman used an erotic voice, another actor sitting to the side said,
What kind of nonsense is this? Those words hardly suit that face!

That and other such insults drew the faintest of smiles upon Shosuke's face.

Tonight's ten-ten-ten sound of pattering rain reminds me I need to pay my respects to ten-Tentoku Temple.

- *The next to come out will be me from the big valley (His name is Otani, meaning the big valley)*
- *Mr. Kinsho you are really on fire tonight!*
- *Thank you Mr. Baju! (a name with Kanji meaning 10 horses but a homonym for horse soup) You are a little too salty for me I'm afraid!*

Note:

According to the notes by the editor of *The Complete Santo Kyoden Volume 2,* several characters in this book are based on real people. Both the hero of this story Ichikawa Shosuke and his friend Kaneko are based on famous Kabuki actors alive at that time. The drawings are actually likenesses of their faces. In addition, the actors in this scene are all likenesses of famous Kabuki actors at that time.

The shouting of salespeople in the intermission is different from the shouting done during performances. In the middle of Kabuki plays die-hard fans known as O-Muko shout out various things at designated times. They will not shout out the actor's name but rather his studio name.

Following the debacle at the theater Shosuke fell upon the notion of spending a 1000 gold coins on a fireworks show. The timing was rather poor as the nighttime temperature was still frigid, but he set out from Nakashu port in a large covered boat. As it turns out even if you launch fireworks all night long, 1000 gold coins in fireworks won't be exhausted by morning. Therefore they decided to begin the show at around noon.

40

The weather was clear that day so, for the residents of Edo, they would hear Boom! Boom! at regular intervals. People for the most part thought it was a shooting star or a falling star and went about their business as normal.

Citizen 1: *I heard some noise from other there, but when I looked there wasn't anything....*Citizen 2: *Who on earth would be setting off fireworks at this time of day?*

Though Shosuke had tried a variety of ways to spend money the "entertainment" ended up being rather dull. He lamented his inability to use his money effectively. "I feel like it's a non-stop battle to rid myself of my accumulated wealth."

Thinking he would leave a legacy of good works behind, Shosuke handed all the poor people in Edo a gold coin in an attempt to spread a little joy.

Since they were untouchables they made no effort to respond with a small gift of their own, but simply said,
Oh thank you! Oh thank you! over and over again in a wholly unconvincing manner.
They added things like:
- *Oh, you in front one more!*
- *Put your hand out like a doggie!*
- *Hello! Hello! There is one more here!*
- *Oh my, oh my! Thank the mountains and the nightingales and the skylarks.*

Note:
非人 Hinin and 穢多 Eta

Edo Era (1603-1868) Japan had a four tier class system Samurai-Farmers-Artisans-Merchants 士農工商. In addition to this there were two classes of "untouchables." The Hinin "non-humans" and the Eta "unclean ones" who were considered outside normal society. Up until the Edo period Hinin was a general term for all such people but starting in the 17th century they made Hinin and Eta separate castes. Hinin were simply poor people or those convicted of minor crimes. Eta butchered large animals, executed prisoners and buried the bodies of criminals. Though the Hinin were technically lower in rank than Eta, Hinin could work their way back to becoming a farmer or city worker. When the system was eliminated in 1871 there were about 23,000 registered in this class.

Image of an Eta working with animal hides from the 1808 book Songs of the Workers of Edo 江戸職人歌合 by Ishihara Masaakira.

I'm sure you are all familiar with the line from the epic song from the Kabuki play is *What the Grass Taught the Sparrow of Yoshiwara* 教草吉原雀(1768.)

The freeing of all living things, which began in the fall of the 4th year of Yohro, never fails to bring great merit and a divine reward. Note: "A sparrow of Yoshiwara" is any person that frequents the pleasure quarters, and is therefore knowledgeable about who also regularly visits that area.

Shosuke began participating in Hojoe, or the Buddhist Rescuing the Lives of Animals Society. He went all around Edo buying eels, turtles and sparrows then freed them. Since that didn't seem to be going far enough he went to eel restaurants and freed the ones they kept alive. He also purchased and released the carp being kept alive on Mukai Island (Mukai Island was famous for its carp restaurants and was located close to the Yoshiwara district.)

Shosuke:
Though my money may die here, it will result in life being able to live free. This has not been money spent in vain.

He also freed the herons in Anjincho (modern day Nihonbashi. Named after William Adams 1564-1620 the man the book *Shogun* by James Cavell was based on.)

Heron: *The money might be better spent buying out courtesans in the Yoshiwara district and freeing them, would be a better "Rescuing the Lives Society."*

I don't really care about rescuing goldfish or Medaka (a small fish that lives in rice paddies.) Since this guy won't kill anything, he shouldn't have any problems in the afterlife.

Note: This scene is also shown on the cover of Volume 2

Cover of Volume 3 of 3

Note: The cover of the 3rd volume shows a man riding a fish, this is Kinko Sennin 琴高仙人 The Taoist Immortal "Master of the Zither." The Taoist Immortal Master of the Zither is a deity that made his way over from China, where he is known as Qin Gao. He was originally a painter of fish. One day a giant carp appeared and transported him to the realm of the immortal. He returned from that journey enlightened to the inner mysteries of Taoism. He is often depicted riding a great fish. on the back of the magical fish.

Image of Master of the Zither depicted as a Courtesan of the Yoshiwara District. 艶中八仙琴高 By Kitagawa Utamaro I

By this point the majority of Shosuke's money had fluttered away on the wind in various entertainments, however a fair amount still remained. Since he had made up his mind to not leave any money behind before he died. Therefore to avoid becoming lost in the afterlife he decided to offer his remaining gold to build a modest grave.

As for his wife, if she did not become a nun it would affect his afterlife adversely. So, despite her protests, she received the tonsure from the head priest and became a nun.

Priest:
With this offering of money, we will offer memorial prayers in perpetuity. Infinite Life Sutra 無量寿経 *May my sincere prayers for my soul allow me to enter the kingdom of heaven. By taking this vow you will be able to board the boat that will take you across the sea to the shore of enlightenment.* Note: This is called Guzei no Fune 弘誓の船 in Japanese.) You will be redeemed in the next life.

Wife:
My precious hair, how tragic! If I had kept this hair and gone to Yoshiwara I could easily have ensnared six men in their bedclothes.
Note: The phrasing of this statement somewhat resembles the phrasing of the scripture.

Lion dog painting:
Not sure if that counts as scripture….

Notes:

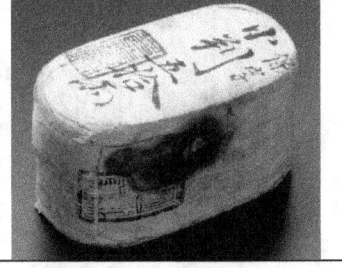

The small packages are Tsutsumi-kin, stacks of 50 Ryo (gold coins) wrapped in paper and sealed with official signatures and stamps guaranteeing the amount. Each oblong coin was worth roughly 1300$. Each stack is about $65,000. Gold Ryo coins were used until the New Currency Act of 1871 when they were replaced with the new monetary unit, Yen.

Samurai were required to wear a long and short sword. When meeting someone the sword was placed on the right hand side with the blade facing you. This would be the most difficult position to draw from.

The grave is called a Bodhi and written 檀那寺 with Kanji that phonetically spell Bodhi in Japanese. The author uses the alternate Kanji 旦那寺 with the same reading but the meaning is "husband shrine." This picture is of the 14th Tokugawa Shogun, Tokugawa Iemochi's grave.

It is said that a person only lasts for one generation but their name lasts forever. That is why leaving a good reputation behind is important. So with that in mind Shosuke ordered copies of his death poem printed out. In addition he inquired of his friends and acquaintances to see if they needed to take revenge on anyone close to them. He promised to use the power of his money to acquire the tools necessary to complete the job. *This is the article I require…*his friend said. *I understand…* replied Shosuke.

Note: Jisei Death Poem

弓取りの数にいるその身となれば 惜しま
ざりけり夏の夜の月

Jisei, which means "A message as I depart this world," is written as a person feels death is approaching. It can also be written before committing Seppuku as shown in the illustration above. The illustration by Tsukioka Yoshitoshi shows Akashid Gidafu 明石儀太夫 (likely a retainer of Akechi Mitsuhide) reviewing his Jisei before committing Seppuku, having failed in battle.

Recalling the number of times I have drawn my bow as a Samurai, giving up my life is as easy as looking up at the summer moon.

Shosuke had managed to rid himself of all of his money through various endeavors. Since the physiognomist had told him that he would die tomorrow at sunset, he was in the lowest of possible moods.

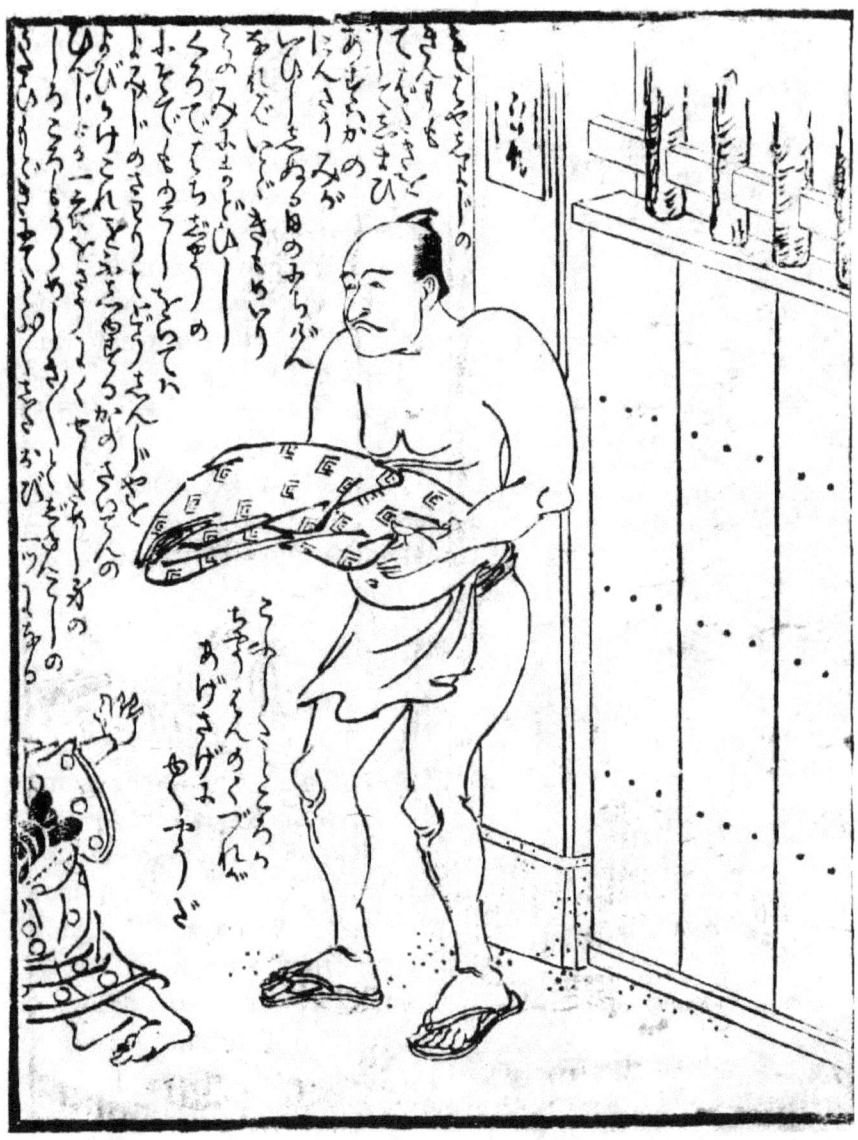

I have no need of this material I've wrapped around my body, however simply abandoning it may hinder me on my way to the other realm.

So, he called out to a Buddhist priest who was proselytizing and gave the clothing to him and asked him to perform the traditional Sutra chant that accompanies donations.

The poor orphan girl of Saiten tried to get the monk to donate the clothing to her. *All I have to wear are these worn out threads, I want them so! I want them so!*

And she began to sing the Noh song the Natural Scholar as Shosuke stripped down to his underwear.

With this look people will think I am going to run a dice game...Taking praise and getting all the blame!

Note:

The dice game is probably *Chō-Han* (丁半) which was a popular form of gambling. The game uses two six-sided dice, which are shaken in a bamboo bowl by a dealer. The cup is then overturned onto the floor. Players then bet on whether the sum total of numbers showing on the two dice will be Chō 丁 (even) or Han 半 (odd.) The dealer then removes the cup, displaying the dice. The winners collect their money. The dealer typically wears only a Fundoshi loin cloth, to avoid accusations of cheating. These men were frequently heavily tattooed.

Orphan girl:
Oh my Oh my! Scary! He looks like a monster!

Priest:
A devout believer! A devout believer! Off to make a pilgrimage up Mt. Hakone!?

Man walking by:
I think you may be mistaken....

Note: The priest has a painting showing a person being judged in hell.

So then, the day of Shosuke's death arrived and he accepted his fate thinking, *now is my time, now is my time…* However, nothing happened that day. Nor the next day. In fact, five days later he was still around. A fortnight later nothing had changed. After a month, still nothing.

Quite unbelievably even after a year there seemed to be no indication that he would soon perish. It seemed as if he had been handed the wrong bill at a restaurant.

He was now far from bored. He was outraged that the money he had frittered away could not be recovered. He now had no choice but to wear a grass mat in place of clothing. For the first time in his life he regretted setting himself on this course so quickly.

It's far too late to try and complain that the physiognomist's prediction was wildly inaccurate, much like when you pick hot peppers too late in the season and then complain they have no flavor!

Advertisement:
Acupuncture without taking your clothes off!

The beggars that Shosuke had given gold coins to saw him and they immediately prostrated themselves in the deepest possible bow.

Beggar #1:
Oh, he who has lost his souls we wish to repay you, we wish to repay you!
Beggar #2:
I can't tell you how thankful I am.
Beggar #3:
Yes, yes! You, my lord, will have to join our business!

Shosuke began to feel like he could no longer continue to live in this fashion so he decided to end it all. Just as he was readying to throw himself into the embrace of death his friend Kaneyuki appeared and called out to him.

Stop! Thou hast gone too far in this course. Though the physiognomist's prediction sent you astray, the whole problem began due to a slight error by Tentei.

Note: "Slight error" can also refer to "wetting the bed."

Kaneyuki:

This led to your soul being taken by that Ninja. Kaneyuki is not my real name, rather it is Kokin Sennin "Master of the Zither" and I am a Taoist Immortal. I vow to use my Senjutsu (Taoist Immortal Power) to restore you.

From inside his breast pocket he removed a flaming ball.
You will become a great man in the future, so you needn't fret over trifles like this.
With that he hurled the flaming soul into Shosuke's mouth, making him whole. Further, the Taoist immortal known as Master of the Zither gave him a poem written on a Tanzaku, a long, narrow card.
The card said,

Start with 9 trees and then add 1 fire from 3 mountains,
To this add 1 measure of soil and 7 parts of the gold you wish to receive.

Shosuke thought about the meaning of this poem for a long time.

Start with 9 trees,
And then add 1 fire from 3 mountains,
To this add 1 measure of soil,
And 7 parts of the gold you wish to receive.

Shosuke came up with the answer in the following way:

Considering the Kanji for tree 木 can be said to be comprised of the Kanji for 8 八 and the Kanji 10 十, adding 9 to that gives you 27 (8+10+9=27.)

Next, taking the Kanji for fire 火 and, add 3 Mountains 山 to it. The Kanji for fire 火 can be said to comprise 2 of the Kanji for 8 八. Three sets of two 8's is 48. (8+8+8+8+8+8=48). Next we have 1 一 measure of earth/soil 土. This Kanji can be said to comprise of the Kanji for 10 十 and 1 一 with that extra mark giving us 十三 13. (1 measure of soil, soil is 10 and 1 plus 1 for the mark.)

Finally, the 7 is the estimated amount of gold so I will add that to what I already have meaning 95.

Realizing this number had special significance he immediately decided to test his luck. I will use this poem, which is part of my soul, as a guide as I record the annals of my life.

Note: This is all imaginative play with Kanji and words. It does not actually the true way Kanji are constructed.

Shosuke took that number 95 as his special number and no matter where he went in Edo he used it to strike riches. He soon found himself wealthy again and he used the money to buy back his land, his house and all his furniture.

As for his wife, who he had sent to the nunnery prematurely, he summoned her back. At first she had to paint her head black and wear a wig, however soon his household was blessed. In fact, he reached an almost unparalleled level of boundless joy. (This seems to imply they had children.)

In deference to the Taoist Immortal Master of the Zither, Shosuke took the image of a carp leaping up a waterfall as his sigil of his house.

"Let's have a drink to our success!"

A Work by Kyoden

Bibliography:
The Complete Santo Kyoden Volume 2 山東京伝全集
第二巻 1993 Edited by Mizuno Minoru 水野稔

三千歳成云蟒蛇

THE GREAT SERPENT TURNS 3,000 YEARS OLD

PUBLISHED 1787

Story: Santo Kyoden 山東京伝, 1761~1816
Art: Hosoda Eishi 細田栄之, 1756~1829
Translation: Eric Shahan シャハン・エリック 1974~

Cover of Volume 1

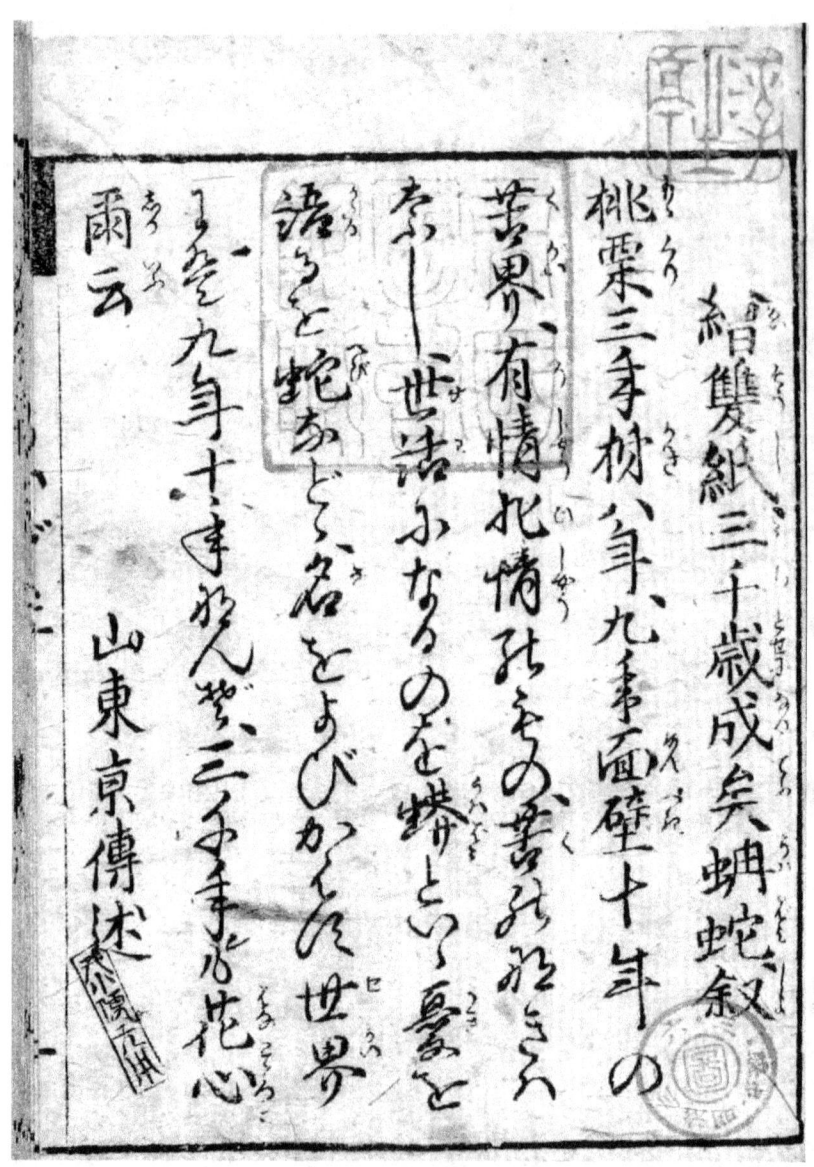

桃栗三年柿八年九年面壁十年の

苦界、有情非情其の苦み皆さ云

志し一世話かなりのを探りとて臺と

語るを蛇あどく名とよびかく世界

一臺九年十年がん梦三の手花心

爾云

絵双紙三十歳成矣蚰蛇叙

山東京傳述

It is said that it takes 3 years for peach trees and chestnut trees to bear fruit and 9 years for a persimmon tree. Staring at a wall for 9 years will enable you to achieve enlightenment and the longest employment contract allowed by the government is ten hard years. In short, all things great and small suffer hardships.

The story of a great serpent on the cusp of change. Even if you were to call this creature a snake for 9 or 10 years, that's nothing in comparison to the 3 millennia of change it has seen.

A story by Santo Kyoden.

No Urinating Here/ No Reading Without Buying

Notes:

- 桃栗三年柿八年 *It takes 3 years for peach trees and chestnut trees to bear fruit and 9 years for a persimmon tree*. The aphorism also means "It takes time for things to come to fruition.

- 九年面壁 *Staring at a wall for nine years* Refers to when the Great Priest Daruma 達磨大師 [?～528] sat facing the wall of a cave in Shorin Temple 少林寺, achieving enlightenment after 9 years.

- 苦界十年 *Ten Hard Years* refers specifically to the longest possible contract duration allowed by the Edo Era government. However it also referred to the length of time a girl had to work as a courtesan in a brothel. Girls were often entered a contract around 16 or 17 and so were bound until around 27 years old.

- 小便无用 Underneath Santo Kyoden's name he wrote "No Urinating Here" with an illustration of a Torii Gate. This was a common sign posted in front of temples and shrines warning the ubiquitous palanquin drivers not to use the gate to the temple as a de-facto toilet. However, another meaning of the phrase is, "No reading without buying."
The Kanji 小便 mean "small use" referring to urination. The is opposed to 大便 which means "big use" referring to defecation. Kyoden is using the "small use" as using his shop as a library instead of a bookstore.

The 4ᵗʰ century BCE book *Classic of Mountains and Seas* contains the line,

After spending 1000 years in the mountains and 1000 years in the sea and 1000 years in a village a Great Serpent will change into a dragon and rise up to the heavens.

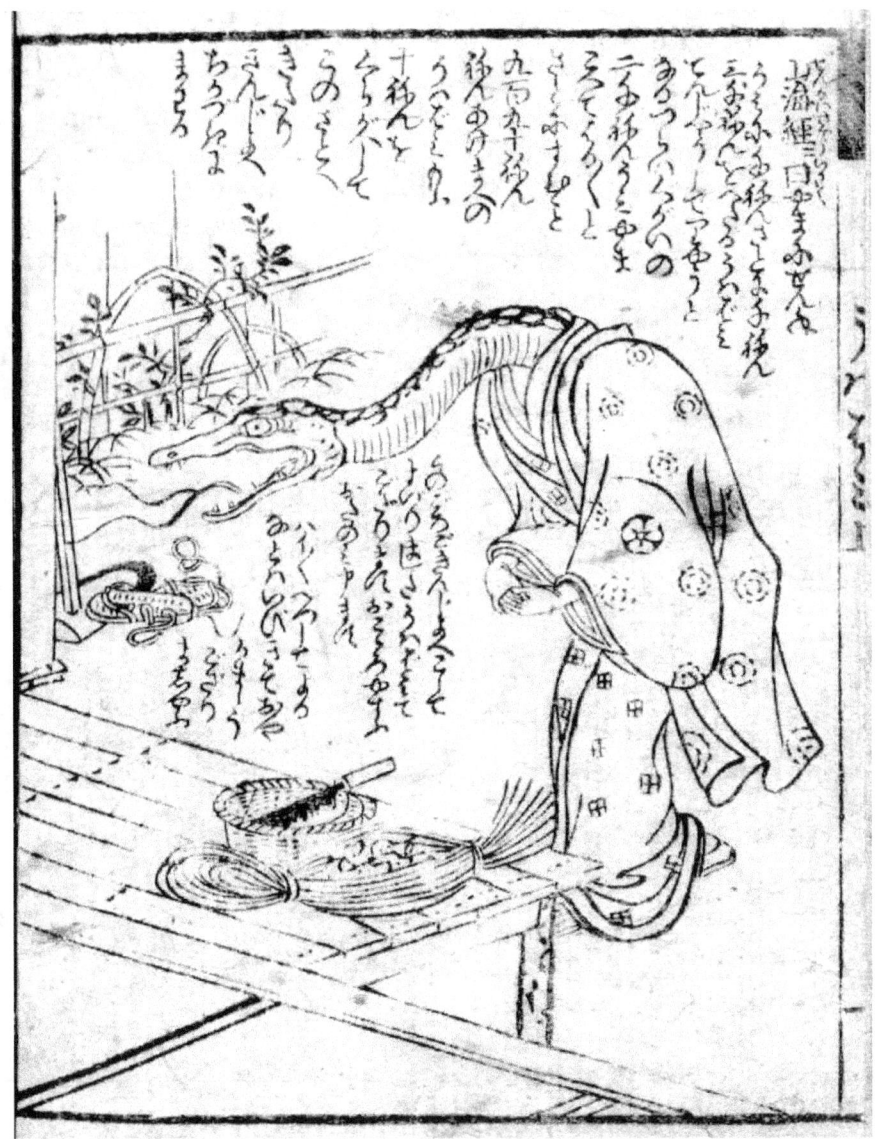

Having endured the torments of the sea and mountains for 2,000 years the great serpent had travelled a great distance to a human village and lived there for 990 years. However, he felt the need to slough off his skin and go to a new village for the next 10 years. After moving to this village he drew close to the people and went around greeting his new neighbors.

Great Serpent:
I've recently moved to the area and thought I might make a small intrusion to introduce myself. I am the Great Serpent. Please don't hesitate to ask if I can be of assistance.

Husband:
That's very nice, that's very nice.

Wife:
Just want to let you know that my snoring can be tremendously loud.

Great Serpent:
Not at all not at all!
I am still in the process of straightening up my grotto, please excuse my mess.

Notes:

- The *Classic of Mountains and Seas* is a compilation of animals and geography both real and mythical. The earliest edition dates from the 4th century BCE but it continued to be adapted through the 2nd century CE. The author is unknown.

- 海千山千 Umisen-Yamasen *After spending 1000 years in the mountains and 1000 years in the sea and 1000 years in a village a Great Serpent will change into a dragon and rise up to the heavens* is an expression that says a snake must live 1000 years in the ocean and a 1000 years in the forest and mountains before it can become a dragon. Another version is that there are actually two snakes. One lives in the mountains and one in the ocean. After spending a thousand years in that area they come together and combine into a dragon. The expression also refers to a person who is sharp-witted, though in a cunning sense so it is not a compliment. It is not clear if Santo Kyoden adds "1000 years in a village" to this or it is an alternate version.

Shoya Ja-Goemon convened the monthly village elders' council. They hadn't heard much from The Great Serpent and were considering whether to send some kind of welcome gift. As it turned out the Serpent had crept up rather close, so the council invited him in.

You've spent quite a long time in the oceans and mountains! I'm sure you've had your share of thrilling and terrifying experiences. Just like The Tale of Rokubu, everyone is very interested in hearing all about it.

So just like a blind masseuse playing the Shamisen (lute) the council showed no fear of the Serpent and sipped their tea contentedly.

Great Serpent:
I know you are all squeezed by your stipends. I, on the other hand, often suffocate my prey with my coils. I also have some troubles of my own. Sometimes when I am taking a nap, a traveler will come along and sit on me, thinking I am the branch of a pine tree. If I open my eyes the person would be frightened so I lay there with my eyes close feigning sleep. It is almost as hard as waiting in the alley beside a famous theater for a prostitute to come by. Stressful indeed. Typically, people are very frightened of me so I rarely make friends in villages.

Head of Elder Council:
My dear Lord Giant Serpent, we thought garnished Tofu and rice dishes would be to your liking, would you perhaps care for a skewer of grilled red frog?

Great Serpent:
I have to say I am very flattered by your hospitality. Please give my regards to the cook!

Notes:

Ja-Goemon: The name Goemon is famous mainly because of the bandit Ishikawa Goemon who was boiled alive with his son as punishment for criminal activity, which consisted of Robin Hood style "steal from the rich and give to the poor." The Ja is the Kanji for Snake 蛇 so his name is "Snake" Goemon. The researcher Minakata Kumagusu 南方 熊楠 (1867-1941) writes in his 1914 book *Reflections on the Stems and Branches* 十二支考 found that colloquially the name Ja-Goemon was intoned over and over whenever a person was bitten by a snake as a protective spell. It derives from Jajo Ieomon 蛇除伊右衛門, "Snake Remover" Iemon.

六部殺し Rokubu: The Tale of Rokubu often called *The Killing of Rokubu* is a folk tale involving a traveler who is murdered by the hosts who took him in for the night.

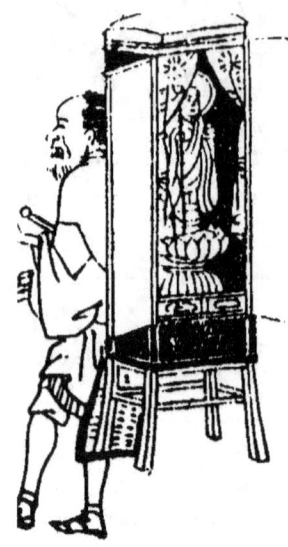

Summary of the of Rokubu:

Rokubu (the name means Six Parts) is the word of a kind of travelling monk. "Rokubu" is an abbreviation for Rokujurokubu (66 Parts) a monk who dedicated himself to copying the Lotus Sutra 66 times and then completing a pilgrimage to 66 spiritual sites to donate one copy to each. Other variations of the story say he is a Takuhatsuzo 托鉢僧 (mendicant monk who practices begging like the illustration to the left,) a travelling salesmen or even a blind masseuse/acupuncturist.

There are numerous other variations. For example:

A Rokubu monk requests lodging at a house of meager means. He is accepted in however at some point during the visit the hosts discover that Rokubu has a large amount of money on him. They decide to kill him, hide the body and take his money.

The family invests the money wisely and become successful. Later, they are blessed with a son, however he never learns to speak. One moonless night a light rain fell and the boy wakes up and begins moving about so the father takes him to the toilet. Suddenly, for the first time the child speaks, "You killed me on a night like this." Following this revelation that the child is the reborn Rokubu, the family business fails and they fall into misery.

Another version of the story tells of a family having a Rokubu pilgrim staying overnight, only to kill him and get his money - and then suffer some kind of curse for generations. The other type of legend tells of families which have a problem and ask an itinerant Rokubu, almost like a Shaman, for explanation, understanding and help.

Mönche von der Sekte Rokubo.

An illustration of Japanese Rokubu travelling monks done by Fredric Shoberl (1775-1853.)

Love always seems to move in unpredictable ways. In this village, there was a girl by the name of O-Kiku, Little Chrysanthemum, the likes of which could be found neither in Edo nor Kyoto. Her smart eyes and smart body movements captured the heart of Ja Goemon's only child, his son Soshiro. Neither of them ever confessed their love and not a single letter was written between them, yet somehow they naturally ended up together.

This is what is known as falling in love naturally.

Little Chrysanthemum: *I talked this over to my friends and they said we should elope together. I can't admit that I want so do something as wicked as that so I will just say, Soshiro! Soshiro!*

Soshiro: T*hough I am betrothed to another, I have no interest in her.*

As the new year began The Giant Serpent twisted himself painfully into the shape of the Kanji 名 (name.)

He mused, *If I am indeed going to rise up the heavens my hands and feet will become covered with rough scales and my hidden claws will have to grasp a great pearl orb.*

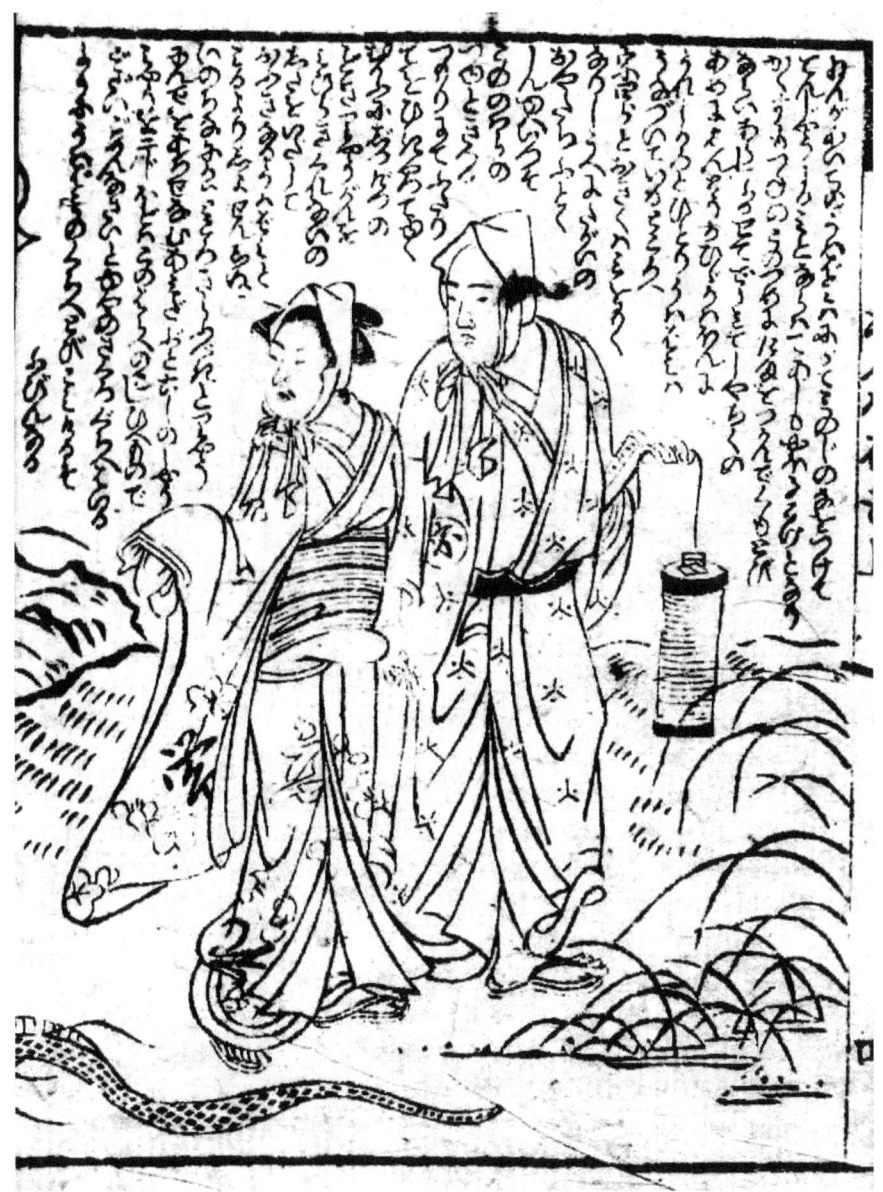

He nodded to himself in delight as he thought about flying up between the clouds, scowling in the face of hurricane force winds and rejoicing at the shuddering impact of rain as heavy as the axle of an ox cart.

In the midst of this revelry, Soshiro and a very pregnant Little Chrysanthemum came by. They had both defied their parents and continued their relationship. They couple had decided to vanish from the village as dew on the field does in the late morning sun. The two, hand in hand, moved across the field directly in front of the Great Serpent. The Serpent had been in the midst of his revelry for many days and months. Seeing the giant snake with its crimson tongue flicking out, the two young people were sure their lives were over, and they would die. Though the sight horrified them they brought their hands together in the six word prayer to the Buddha Na-Mu-A-Mi-Da-Butsu 南無阿弥陀仏.

The first two words hung in the air of that field as they crouched and threw themselves into the yawing mouth of the great serpent which was open like the persimmon door of a bath. And thus, ended their unfortunate lives.

Notes:

- In Asian legends and myths dragons and pearls are closely linked One early Chinese myth related that pearls fell from the sky when dragons fought amongst the clouds. Another myth states that pearls originated as raindrops swallowed by oysters. In one ancient tale, a boy found a miraculous pearl. When placed in a jar with just a bit of rice, it filled the jar with rice the next day. After his neighbors discovered this, they tried to steal it. The boy swallowed the pearl to protect it. Source: www.gemsociety.org

- 南無阿弥陀仏 Namu Amida Butsu : Means *I take refuge in Amida Buddha*." The famous Buddhist Priest Hōnen (1133–1212) of the Pure Land school of Buddhism, asserted chanting this phrase was enough to attain rebirth in the Pure Land. This allowed anyone to achieve enlightenment without intensive study of complicated texts.

- " The persimmon door" (Zakuroguchi 石榴口) was a low door separating two areas of a public bath. It served to prevent the water in the bath from cooling.

Illustration of a persimmon door from the 1773 book by Inkyo Kawa 吟咄川. *When going to the Sento (public bath) they crawl naked under the persimmon door.*

There was a riot going on inside the stomach of the
Serpent. Even if he were to consume some magic concoction of
herbs and grasses it would go unnoticed in the tumult.
The couple bemoaned their situation, *This tragic world! Why did
we have to end up being swallowed by this giant snake?*

Just as their misery was reaching its zenith, Ja-Goemon came running up to the Giant Serpent in tears. However, the Serpent soothed him by saying,
You can relax, they are safe inside my stomach.

Upon hearing this Ja-Goemon replied,
Thank goodness it was my neighbor the serpent that swallowed my son and his lover!
Note: The Kanji "Go"五 is written on the back of Ja-Goemon's shirt for easy identification.

Great Serpent:
My stomach is fit to burst, I am in agony!

The Great Serpent accompanied Ja-Goemon to his residence. Once there, a doctor was summoned to administer a medicinal draught to cause vomiting. The Great Serpent heaved up and spit out first Little Chrysanthemum and then Sojiro. People who heard the story later might have ended up with the mistaken belief that a child was born from the mouth of a snake.

Retching sound, Retching sound

Note:
Kampo Chinese Medicine in Japan

The pharmacist in the background is mixing various dried plant and animal parts together to make Kampo, traditional Chinese medicine as adapted to Japan. Below is a rough outline of when Kampo medicine came to Japan and how it differs from Chinese medicine.

Kampo is a traditional therapeutic system of Japan. Han dynasty's ancient Chinese medicine found its way into Japan, but since its ingredients was hard to find in Japan, it developed its own style. For example, abdominal examination is Kampo's original way of consulting patients. The way they provide prescription is originally Japanese too. The goal of Western medicine is to heal sickness itself, but Kampo attempts to heal the person who is affected by the sickness. Even if patients have the same sickness, their medicine varies depending on the constitution of their bodies or whether they are sensitive to cold or not. The degree of individualization is very different between China and Japan.

Chinese Kampo *is based on herbal medicine, in which optional herbs are mixed, according to each symptom. On the other hand, Japanese* Kampo *is based on prescription. Herbal medicine— which amount is decided in advance—is mixed based on the prescription. Then a couple of doses are arranged accordingly. Research on* Kampo *made progress in the Edo Era, in which original Japanese prescriptions were developed. In addition, Japan placed value on abdominal examination that was not occurred in China, which later influenced China and South Korea.*
Source: Premium Japan www.premium-j.jp

It is said that even the smallest insect has 5% the soul of a human. I can't really say how much of a soul a great serpent has.

The children of humans often play with snakes, ignoring their responsibilities. However, great serpents on the other hand, despise endlessly playing, thus he decided to start some sort of business.

With the help of Ja-Goemon he started doing decorative embroidery. As it turns out the Great Serpent was rather adept at this. It is around this time that the snake-belly scale patter was introduced to the world.

Due to the good graces and tutelage of Kyu-Hyoei of Tamachi Village, Edo, the Great Serpent became a sought-after embroidery artist.

Kyu-Hyoei:
We've come up with a great plan! All the courtesans at the Chojiha Inn will wear this pattern.

Great Serpent:
Isn't it about time we stopped for lunch? I think we've piled up quite a mountain today.

Notes:

- Santo Kyoden was famous for including likenesses of his friends and contemporary celebrities (like Kabuki actors) in his works. Kyu-Hyoei is one such person who owned an embroidery shop in Edo. Kyu-Hyoei was a friend of Kyoden and even helped negotiate Kyoden's marriage to his second wife, a courtesan from the Yoshiwara red light district. It cost 20 gold coins to buy out her contract.

- The artist was a Samurai who worked for the Bakufu government but managed to extricate himself from that job by transferring his position to his adopted son. This allowed him to pursue his carrier as a comic book artist which no doubt horrified his mother.

With the coming of the New Year, courtesans can end their contracts. Of course, they must pay back their loans and leave an appropriate souvenir for the tea house (some tea houses offer more than tea,) the assistants and apprentice assistants, the guards and the guardhouse and finally the younger courtesans and the courtesan's assistants. That is why you don't often hear of courtesans leaving Yoshiwara.

However, it is not just courtesans going about handing out New Year's gifts but Great Serpents as well. Since he was going to transform into a dragon and rise to the heavens, he would no doubt wreak havoc on the local fields and small buildings.

Uwabami, The Great Serpent, had made good use of the money he had saved over the course of 3,000 years.

I have to make sure all my accounts are in order….Just like a courtesan I plan to leave this shop tomorrow. Some people are probably scheming to make use of that knowledge…
What to do…What to do….

If I was staying on this mortal world, I could lend this money out. If the borrower tried to wriggle out of paying me back I could just say, "I'll sprinkle salt on your head and swallow you whole!"

Note:

Yoshiwara

Yoshiwara was the official red-light district of Edo that served both city dwellers as well as Samurai. The number of women there at any one time varied from 1,700 to 3,000 over the course of the Edo Era 1600-1868. Girls from poor families would work as servants starting at the age of 7-12. Girls working as courtesans would start a 10 year contract at the age of 16 or 17. Theoretically their contract would end at 27 or 28 but due to debt occurred for such things as taking days off and absences due to illness, the official contract would be extended. Some women were able to buy their freedom but others could not. A wealthy customer could buy out a woman's contract which is what Santo Kyoden did, twice. His first wife was a woman named Kikuen 菊園 when he was around 19 and she was in her mid-20s. She died at around the age of 30. were around 20. At the age of 37 Kyoden married another courtesan named Tama No-E 玉の井

Interior view of a brothel in the Yoshiwara District.
By Torii Kiyonaga 鳥居清長 1787

Counting each of the 10 years an Oiran (a high class courtesan) works in the savage world of the courtesan is like breaking a finger for each year. While that agonizing long time was the same as the duration of the Great Serpent's stay in the village, that span was but a trifle to him.

In fact, 12 years flew by and he was two years past 3,000 years. Since it was past time for him to rise up into the sky he offered his resignation and went around the village wishing everyone farewell.

Ja-Goemon, Soshiro and Little Chrysanthemum owed a lot to the Great Serpent and wanted something to remember him by.

Ja-Goemon:
When the clouds are passing and the wind shakes the ground we may be able to catch a brief glimpse of the Great Serpent.

The whole village turned out to see Uwabami, the Great Serpent, ascend. They had become friendly with him over the past dozen years and they did not want him to leave the village.

Soshiro and Little Chrysanthemum:
If ever a great storm blows in, we can use that as a chance to have a brief reunion with you! Sayonara! I hope your rise to heaven goes smoothly and quietly!

Great Serpent:
As I go up undoubtedly strong winds will blow and rain will fall!

The third generation Ozatsuma Shuzen Taifu 大薩摩
主膳太夫 (?-1800) Joruri theater actor as The Great Serpent Rising
to Heaven.

Once amongst the clouds many interesting things were written but as it was dark they couldn't be read.

Note: This two page illustration resembles the type of scene that could be found painted on a temple ceiling. The symbol at the top right is the three claws of a dragon holding a pearl orb.

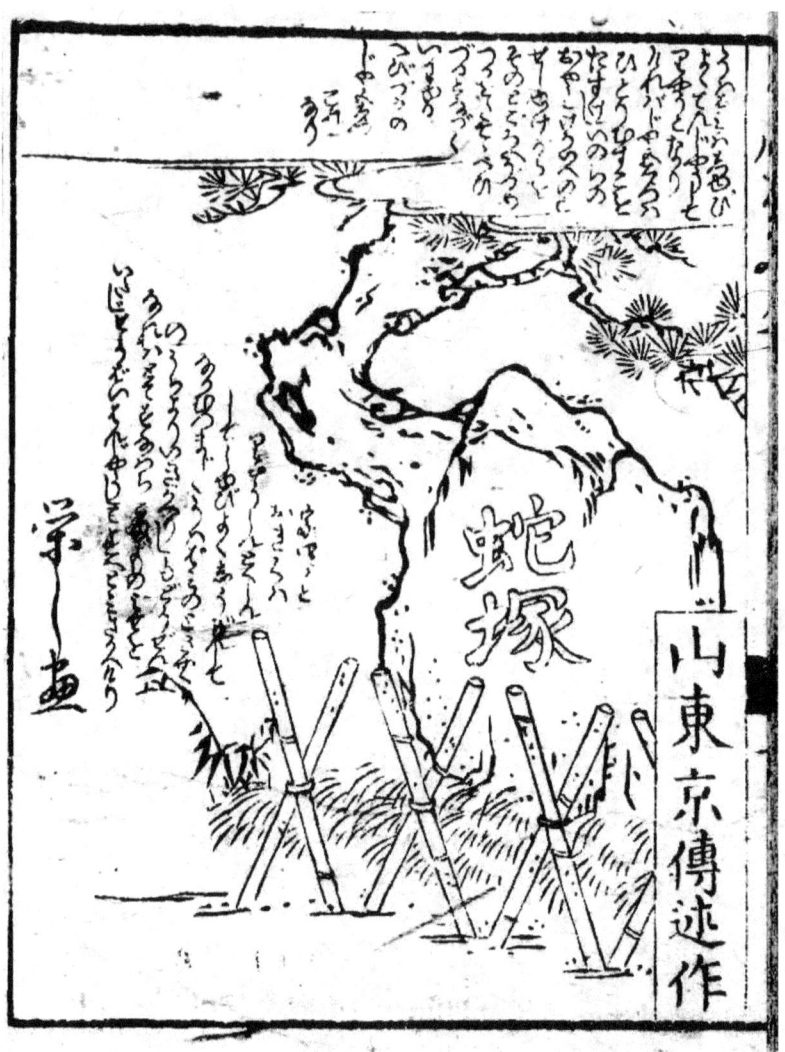

So Uwabami, the Great Serpent, transformed into a dragon and rose effortlessly up to the heavens. Ja-Goemon felt deeply indebted to him for saving his son and when he found the skin shed by the snake and left on the mortal world during his transformation, he collected and buried it. On top of this he built a mound and called it Hebi-zuka, Snake Hill. He became known as Ja-Goemon of Snake Hill.

Soshiro and Little Chrysanthemum took their parents words to heart and offered prayers of thanks that their adventure had ended safely. Their union was harmonious, and it was like they were reborn after having been vomited up by the Giant Serpent. They opened a small dry goods shop and their sales were brisk and in the end the found good fortune and success followed them.

A Work by Kyoden
Art by Eishi

Bibliography:
The Complete Santo Kyoden Volume 2 山東京伝全集 第二巻 1993 Edited by Mizuno Minoru 水野稔

Cover of Volume 2

Note:
Hebizuka is an actual place in Tokyo and was considered a "power spot" for people that wanted good fortune regarding marriage and having children. Offerings of Sake and eggs were common. When I visited the whole area was being renovated however an acquaintance was there a few years before and had some shots.

Then:

Photo credit:
John Anderson, Jinenkan Tatsumaki Dojo

Now:

Pictures of a 2019 renovation that is scheduled to be completed in late 2020.

www.ingramcontent.com/pod-product-compliance
Lightning Source LLC
Chambersburg PA
CBHW071409170626
46811CB00003B/1320

* 9 7 8 1 9 5 0 9 5 9 0 7 5 *